CHICKEN SOUP for LITTLE SOULS

A Dog of My Own

Story by
Lisa McCourt

Illustrated by
Katya Krenina

Health Communications, Inc.
Deerfield Beach, Florida

Library of Congress Cataloging-in-Publication Data

McCourt, Lisa.
    Chicken soup for little souls : a dog of my own / story by Lisa McCourt ; illustrations by Katya Krenina.
        p.   cm.
    "Inspired by the #1 New York times best-selling series Chicken soup for the soul."
    Summary: Ben rescues a dog who is afraid of everything and uses love and patience to earn his
confidence and bring out his good qualities.
    ISBN 1-55874-555-6 (hardcover)
    [1. Dogs—Fiction. 2. Pets—Fiction.]
    I. Krenina, Katya, ill. II. Title.
    PZ7.M47841445Cl   1998
    [Fic]—dc21   97-30906
                                                                                             CIP
                                                                                              AC

Story inspired by *Chicken Soup for the Soul*®, edited by Jack Canfield and Mark Victor Hansen.

Story ©1998 Lisa McCourt
Illustrations ©1998 Katya Krenina

Cover Design by Cheryl Nathan

The author wishes to thank Caroline Crane-Thomason, Director of Education at the Humane Society of Broward
County, for sharing her animal wisdom.

Produced by Boingo Books, Inc.

Publisher: Health Communications, Inc.
            3201 S.W. 15th Street
            Deerfield Beach, FL 33442-8190

Printed in Mexico

For Michael and Elizabeth, with love
—L.M.

For Miron, with love
—K.K.

For Christopher, whose unconditional love for Daisy is an inspiration
—J.C.

This book is dedicated to the unconditional love of our best friend
—M.V.H.

For my wife Anne and our children Melinda and Hayley
—P.V.

For my daughter Mandy — and my sons Oliver and Robert
in the hope this will inspire them to open and turn the pages of this precious volume
—G.S.

Mom had barely gotten in the door when I started my pleading again. This time, she flopped down on the sofa and said, "Okay, Ben, but only if it's free and you do everything to take care of it. That means walking it, training it, feeding it...everything."

My mouth dropped open. Okay? She really said okay?

This was only the thousandth time that I had begged for a dog of my own. Every time, Mom had said no. Every time, she had given a different reason why it just wouldn't work.

"Mom?" I crept closer and looked her in the eyes to make sure I wasn't hearing things. "Did you just say I could have a dog?"

Mom hugged me. "Now that school is out, yes. You can have one."

I had never felt so great in my life. I jumped! I yelled! My best-ever wish was coming true!

The next morning I set out with a leash and my best friend, Kelly, for Mr. Hogan's farm. Mr. Hogan's collie, Sunset, was the smartest, most beautiful dog in town and her new litter of pups was going fast. He was charging money for them, but I had been doing chores for him ever since he told me Sunset would be having puppies so he'd give me one for free if I got my mom to say yes.

Kelly and I were about half way to Mr. Hogan's when we heard our neighbor, Old Man Ackerman, yelling in his front yard.

"Come on out here!" Old Man Ackerman hollered at a big, green bush. "I'm not going to hurt you."

I tapped him on the shoulder. "Anything we can do?" I asked.

"Oh! Ben. Kelly. I'm glad you kids are here. Crawl under there and get that scrawny dog for me, will you? He's been running wild around here for over a month, eating what he can from people's garbage. His owners must not want him anymore and some of the neighbors have been complaining about him. I told them I'd bring him to the pound."

"The pound!" said Kelly. "Can't you keep him?"

"I'm too old to take care of a dog and no one else wants him. His name tag says 'Duke,' but the police say no one's reported a missing dog. It's easy to see that his owners treated him badly. He's afraid of just about everything. Most nervous dog I've ever seen."

I looked under the bush and saw two big, scared eyes staring back at me. I didn't even have time to think about what I did next. "Please don't take him to the pound," I said. "I'll take care of him myself."

"What would you want with a creature like that?" Old Man Ackerman asked. "He's scared of his own shadow. Won't let people touch him. Couldn't protect you from an ant."

"Like I said, I'll take him, sir," I repeated. I knew Mom would understand.

"If you want him, he's yours," said Old Man Ackerman. "But if I see him running wild again, I'm going to have to take him to the pound like I promised folks I'd do. Good luck getting him out from under that bush." Old Man Ackerman slowly made his way back to his house.

Kelly and I got down on our bellies and stared at Duke. Then we stared at each other, and back at Duke again. I'd had my heart set for months on one of Sunset's puppies—but how could I let this poor dog end up at the pound?

"You've got to take him," said Kelly. "He needs you."

I knew she was right.

It wasn't easy to get the leash on Duke. He slunk down and scampered deeper under the bush whenever I got close to him. Finally, Kelly and I cornered him and snapped the leash on his collar. His heart raced way too fast as he looked at me with big, chocolate-colored eyes. I gently stroked his head. "It'll be okay now," I whispered in his ear. "You're safe with me."

Walking Duke home was a disaster. At first he wouldn't budge, and Kelly and I had to use all our combined strength to pull him along the side of the road. Then he lunged ahead so fast we thought he'd choke himself. Whenever a car passed, he whirled behind me in fear, wrapping his leash around and around my legs until we were both completely stuck. It wasn't the way I'd always imagined walking my dog.

Kelly's mom took care of me whenever my mom was working, so she was the first to meet Duke and hear the story about why we took him.

"Oh, my," was all Kelly's mom would say. She made a hamburger for us to give Duke, and put some water in a bowl. But the second I took his leash off him, Duke raced to the row of blackberry bushes between my back yard and Kelly's and hid himself underneath the thickest clump.

It was tight, but I crawled under just far enough to pull Duke out. I dragged him to his food, and held him firmly in front of it. I tried to comfort him by petting his head, but his eyes were big and scared, and his tail didn't wag. When I thought maybe he was relaxed enough to eat, I let him go. Zoom! Duke raced right back to his spot under the bushes.

For hours, Kelly and I talked softly to Duke. I laid down on the ground so that I could reach my hand in far enough to stroke his trembling side. It wasn't the way I'd always imagined spending the day with my dog.

Soon Mom was home, calling me in for dinner. But I was afraid to leave Duke. "I'll stay with him while you eat," said Kelly.

While I set the table, I told Mom about my day.

"A dog like that will take a lot of love and a lot of patience," said Mom. "You would have had a much easier time with one of Sunset's puppies."

"I couldn't leave Duke, Mom. He needs me more. Mr. Hogan will find good homes for the puppies. Duke might never have had a good home if I hadn't come along."

After dinner, I looked for Kelly. She was hiding behind a tree a few feet away from Duke, watching him. "What are you doing?" I asked.

"Sssshhhhhh!" she hissed. I looked under the bushes. Duke was eating! Kelly had brought the hamburger and water and left it under there for him.

"If you get too close, he won't eat it," she said.

I hid behind a tree, too. "Thanks, Kelly," I whispered. "That was a great idea."

When he finished eating, I pulled Duke out and dragged him into the house. He trembled in my arms, and when I let go, he scampered under the washstand.

Mom looked at him and shook her head. "Well, he won't win any beauty contests," she said.

"Beauty isn't everything," I told her. "Duke is smart and loyal and brave...or at least he will be when he stops being so scared. Mom, why is he so afraid of me? I would never hurt him. Can't he tell that?"

"Duke has probably had a very hard life. It won't be easy for him to trust people again. The best you can do for a dog like that is give him as much love as you've got and as much time as he needs."

I knew I had plenty of love for Duke. I pulled him out from under the washstand and brought him to my room. I wanted him to sleep on my bed, but he just wedged himself between my desk and the wall and watched my every move with those big, worried eyes.

For the next few weeks, nothing changed with Duke. He still ran and hid whenever he got a chance; he still wouldn't eat if he thought anyone was watching; he still never once barked, or played, or wagged his tail. Twice a day I put his leash on him and tried to take him for a walk, but every noise, passing car, or falling leaf nearly scared him to death.

One day, as Kelly and I were doing our best to walk Duke, we saw Bart Morrison. Bart was walking the collie pup his family had bought from Sunset's litter. The puppy was prancing along like she knew just how wonderful and special she was. When she saw Duke, she playfully barked and pulled Bart toward us.

Poor Duke just about fell over from fear. He wedged himself between my legs and trembled uncontrollably as the two walked by.

"Nice dog," snickered Bart as he passed.

"You bet he is! He's better than your dog any day!" Kelly yelled.

Bart just laughed and took off running with his cinnamon-colored, fluffy, perfect collie. "C'mon, Brandy! C'mon, girl!" he coached as they happily ran off toward the park. I followed them with my eyes until they were just a speck. What a great dog that Brandy was. The kind of dog I could have owned.

I sighed and reached down to try to untangle Duke from my legs. Something warm and wet softly brushed my hand. He licked me! Duke licked me!

"Kelly, did you see that?" I shouted. "Duke licked my hand! He trusts me now! He loves me!"

I got Duke's leash untangled. He still looked scared and worried, but there was something else in his chocolatey eyes. Something a little like hope.

After that lick, I knew Duke was worth waiting for. I stopped thinking about Sunset's puppies and what mine might have been like. I just thought about loving Duke.

As the weeks went by, I got pretty used to the way Duke liked things. I stopped trying to get him to act the way I wanted him to and started accepting him just the way he was. I even put soft pillows in all his favorite safe spots so he could hide out in comfort.

That night, with Duke crouched in his usual corner by my desk, I stretched out on the floor to read a book. I saw Duke peeking at me. Then, slowly, he crept out, getting closer and closer to my side of the room.

Finally, he laid down right beside me, gently leaning his warm body against my leg and resting his chin on my thigh. His tail thump-thumped against the carpet. I gently stroked his head until the lids on his liquidy chocolate eyes peacefully drooped and closed.

Right then and there I knew there was no better dog in the whole wide universe anywhere. Duke still needed love and he still needed time, but he was getting braver and happier every day.

"I'll give you all the love and time in the world," I whispered to my very own dog as he trustingly drifted off to sleep at my side.